To my three little fish

Lauren, Molly, and Bennett

little fish, BIG QUESTION

Written by Angela Willingham   Illustrated by Nevine Younes

Note to Reader

Serving as a volunteer after college, I had a conversation with an amazing man,
Father Clark Yates, a retired priest living in Tenafly, New Jersey.

I can't remember exactly what we were talking about, but I said,
"Well, that's what's wrong with the world today."
He paused for a moment, grinned, and said,
"You are like a fish looking for water."
I asked, "You mean I am a fish out of water?"
And he replied, "Nope. You're in it. You just don't see it."

It took me twenty years to find the water and now I am delighted
to share my journey with you through the story of Little Fish.

"Mom?"

"Yes, Love?"

"Where is the water?"

"You can't *see* it
until you *feel* it.

Let's find it together.
Be still and breathe.

Breathe in....
    ...and out...
        ...and in."

After a few moments Little Fish
opened her eyes and sighed,

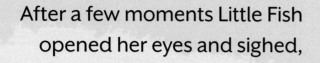

"I still can't feel it."

"Yet,"
Mom replied.

"You can't feel it yet.
It's important that you
never stop searching.

Practice being still
and it will come to you."

"Mom, I'm tired of being still.
Can I go look for the water on my own?"

"Of course,"
Mom answered.

"And on your journey perhaps you
can ask others to show you the way."

"Great idea!"

Little Fish kissed her mom goodbye
and rushed out to find the water.

She began by asking the grumpy old octopus next door.

"Excuse me, ma'am.
    Can you please show me the water?"

The grumpy old octopus
scoffed at such a silly question.

"What do you mean, 'show you the water'?

"Well, my entire life I've heard about the water.
How it is part of us and how we need it to live,
but I can't find it."

The grumpy old octopus
closed her eyes and sighed,

"You're wasting your time.
There is no such thing as water.
Now leave me alone."

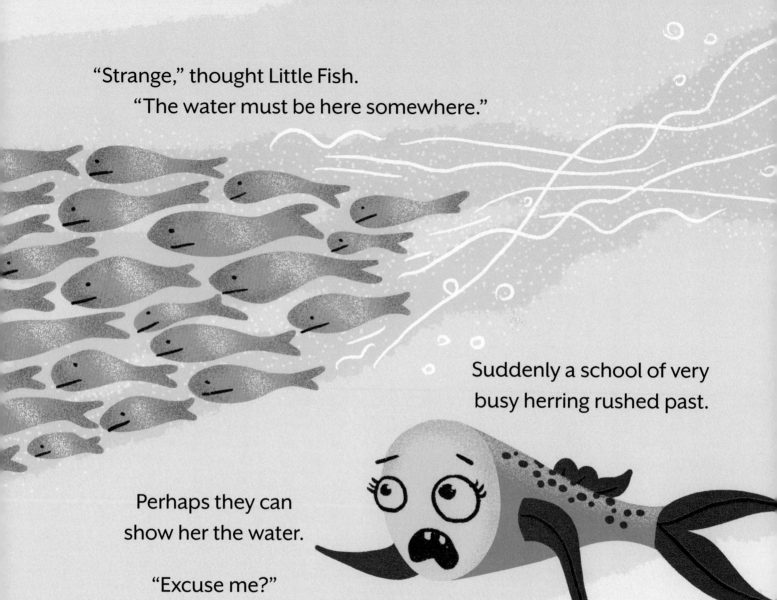

"Strange," thought Little Fish.
"The water must be here somewhere."

Suddenly a school of very
busy herring rushed past.

Perhaps they can
show her the water.

"Excuse me?"

No one answered her, so she cleared her throat
and tried again in a much bolder voice.

One of the very busy herring responded,
   "What do you want?
      Can't you see we are very busy?"

"Oh yes," said Little Fish.
"You look very important,
   so I thought you must
      be looking for the water.

Can I follow you?"

"No, we are far too busy
   to look for the water."

"Well, then, where are you going in such a hurry?"

"I don't know.

I am just following the fish in front of me."

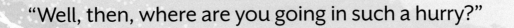

"So how will you know
when you get there?"

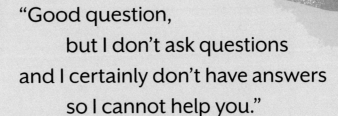

"Good question,
but I don't ask questions
and I certainly don't have answers
so I cannot help you."

Little Fish continued to search

and

all

ask

sorts

of

creatures,

and although some tried,
no one could show her the water.

She remembered her mom's advice—be still and breathe.

Breathe in and out...
and in and out.

After a few moments she opened her eyes,
looked around, and suddenly realized
she didn't know where she was.

"I'm lost!"

Little Fish panicked and began swimming erratically looking for anything familiar.

Then in the distance she saw a creature that she'd never seen before.

Perhaps he can help.

"Excuse me. Can you help me?

I was looking for the water,
but now I don't know
my way back home."

"What do you mean you were
looking for the water?!"
The worm laughed.

"Can't you see it?
The water is all around you."

Tired and frustrated, Little Fish shouted,
   "Don't mock me!
      All my life I have been asking this simple question
         and all I want is a simple answer.

Where is the water?!"

She stared at him a good long while
   and when he didn't answer she swam away.

"Wait!"
He called out.
"I can help you find the water."

"You can?!"
exclaimed Little Fish.

"Yes, but finding the water
is never simple and
you might not make it home.

Do you still want to go?"

"Yes! Please show me the water."

"Well, I can't show it to you,
but I can help you find it.

Just bite this hook and don't let go
no matter what."

Little Fish had never seen a hook.
She looked at it cautiously—not sure if she should trust the worm.

He looked her in the eyes and said,

"Trust me,
you're ready."

She bravely bit the hook
and in a flash was pulled
towards a bright light.

As she broke through the surface
she began thrashing around
gasping for breath.

The fisherman reeled her
in and gripped her tightly.

Little Fish couldn't breathe.

She struggled against his grasp,
but he wouldn't let go.

She tried as hard as she could to break free,
but eventually she remembered her mom's advice
and became very, very still.

The fisherman gently unthreaded the hook
and slowly released his grip to admire his catch.

Suddenly,
  in one quick movement,

she l e a p e d out of his hand

and s p l a s h e d into the water.

As she broke through the surface,
she took a deep breath in.

Startled by what she felt, she opened her eyes and shouted

"I found it!

I found the water!"

She looked around in amazement.
Everything looked so different...
familiar, but different.

Behind her she heard a voice ask,
"Isn't it beautiful?"

"Mom?!"

She rushed into her mom's fins.

"I did it."
Little Fish whispered.
"I went out on my own and I found the water."

Her mom hugged her tightly
and whispered back,

"I always knew you would."

THE END

Balboa Press books may be ordered through booksellers or by contacting:

Balboa Press
A Division of Hay House
1663 Liberty Drive
Bloomington, IN 47403
www.balboapress.com
1 (877) 407-4847

Design and Illustration: Nevine Younes

ISBN: 978-1-9822-4743-0 (sc)
978-1-9822-4744-7 (e)
978-1-9822-5074-4 (hc)

Library of Congress Control Number: 2020910431

Print information available on the last page.

Balboa Press rev. date: 06/19/2020

A DIVISION OF HAY HOUSE

Angela Willingham

lives in Rockville, Maryland with her husband and their three little fish. She found the water after 20 years of searching and now helps others find it, too. Learn more at **needlessjourney.com**

Nevine Younes

is a designer and illustrator who lives in San Diego with her very silly dog, Violet. She designed this book using variations of the typeface Mr Eaves. See more of her work at **nevineyounes.com**

Printed in the United States
By Bookmasters